THE SECOND PRINCESS

First published in Great Britain by
Andersen Press Ltd in 1994
First published in Picture Lions in 1995
10 9
Picture Lions is an imprint of the Children's Division,
part of HarperCollins Publishers Ltd, 77-85 Fulham Palace Road,
Hammersmith, London W6 8JB
Text copyright © Hiawyn Oram 1994
Illustrations copyright © Tony Ross 1994
The author and illustrator assert the moral right to be
identified as the author and illustrator of the work.
ISBN: 0 00 664412 0
Printed and bound in Singapore.

THE SECOND PRINCESS

Hiawyn Oram and Tony Ross

PictureLions

An Imprint of HarperCollins*Publishers*

Once there were two princesses, the First Princess and the Second Princess.
The First Princess liked being first but the Second Princess did not like being second.

So she ran into the woods to find the Grey Wolf.

"Grey Wolf, Grey Wolf," she said, "you must come into the palace at the dead of night and gobble up my sister so that I can be first."

"Goodness, gracious," said the Grey Wolf, "what a wicked thought. I would never do a thing like that. Never."

So the Second Princess went to find the Brown Bear.

"Brown Bear, Brown Bear," she said, "you must come to the palace and marry my sister so she's not at home and I can be first."

"Oh must I, indeed?" said the Brown Bear. "Well, let me tell you, I wouldn't marry your sister if she were the last person on earth. Besides, as you can see, I'm already happily married."

So the Second Princess stamped into the palace kitchens, her face as white as a sheet.
"Cook, Cook," she said, "baked in a pie or gone in a puff of steam, I don't care.
I want my sister out of the way so I can be first and that's an order."

"Very well," said the greedy Cook, "but I shall want something in return."

"Like what?" said the Second Princess.

"Jewels," said the greedy Cook, "your mother's jewels. All of them. Jewels, jewels and more jewels!"

"I'll try," said the Second Princess.

So the Second Princess crept into her mother's bedroom and did what she could
… cramming and stuffing and pocketing glittering gorgeous things …

... lockets, tiaras and watches, necklaces, chokers and chains, bracelets, brooches and earrings, hatpins, buckles and rings ... and though her heart was beating like a loud clock and her knees were trembling like trembly jelly she grew so busy with it ...

. . . she did not notice the Maid come in to make the bed, the Queen come in to find the Maid,

two Ladies-in-Waiting come in to find the Queen, two Guards come in to find the Ladies-in-Waiting,

the Lord High Chamberlain come in to find the Guards, and the King come in to find the Lord High Chamberlain.

In fact, only when the Maid sobbed, the Queen gasped, the Ladies-in-Waiting fainted, the Guards shouted, "Who goes there?" and the King marched her off to the Throne Room did she realise she was caught – in the act and red-handed.

"Well," said the King, when they were alone in the Throne Room. "I am waiting, I am waiting, I am waiting."

But, of course, the one thing in the world the Second Princess could NEVER do was TELL what she had been doing with the Queen's jewels.

All she could do was hang her head and try not to imagine what would happen if anyone ever found out.

At last the Queen swept in with an idea.

"If you cannot tell us what you were doing with the jewels," she said, "then we shall have to guess. Was it to polish them?"

The Second Princess shook her head.

"Was it to play Kings and Queens?" said the King.

The Second Princess shook her head.

"Then was it to give them to someone ..." said the Queen, "in return for something you wanted ... very, very much?"

And then and only then did the Second Princess put her hands over her eyes so she could only half be seen and whisper so softly through her fingers that the King and Queen had to come very close to hear.

"Yes ..." came the soft whisper. "So ... that ... I ... could ... be ... first."

And to her great surprise the sky did not fall in and the world did not come to an end. Instead the Queen sighed gratefully and the King said, "Thank goodness we know, now run along and help your mother put away her tiaras ..."

"…and from now on you will be first on Mondays, Wednesdays and Fridays…"
which she was,

"and the First Princess will be first on Tuesdays, Thursdays and Saturdays . . ."
which she was,

"and on Sundays we'll all be first," said the King. And they were.

And though the First Princess took a while getting used to not being first all of the time, and the Second Princess took a while getting used to being first some of the time, and Sundays were always a bit of a bunfight, they all lived very happily afterwards,

except for the Cook, who stormed off in a huff because all she wanted was jewels, jewels and more jewels and because she never knew which day of the week it was, anyway.

Hiawyn Oram was born and brought up in Johannesburg, South Africa. She graduated in English and Drama and acted professionally before moving to Britain. Since then, Hiawyn has had a variety of jobs in London – from cooking for film studios to writing television commercials.

Tony Ross has collaborated with her on JENNA AND THE TROUBLEMAKER, ANYONE SEEN HARRY LATELY and RECKLESS RUBY, and Satoshi Kitamura has also illustrated several of Hiawyn's books.

She currently lives in London with her two sons, Maximilian and Felix.

Tony Ross was born in London in 1938. His dream was to work with horses but instead he went to art college in Liverpool. Since then, Tony has worked as an art director at an advertising agency, a graphic designer, a cartoonist, a teacher and a film maker – as well as illustrating over 250 books! Tony, his wife Zöe, and family live in Macclesfield, Cheshire.

Picture Lions by Tony Ross
I WANT MY POTTY • I WANT TO BE • SUPER DOOPER JEZEBEL
THE KNIGHT WHO WAS AFRAID OF THE DARK
JENNA AND THE TROUBLEMAKER • RECKLESS RUBY